SHADOWS IN THE LIGHT OF A PALE MOON

THE STORY OF BENNY ACKERMAN
MISTAKES MADE & LESSONS LEARNED
IN SELF-DEFENSE

JOHN MARINELLI

Shadows In The Light of A Pale Moon
The Benny Ackerman Story
(Mistakes Made & Lessons Learned In Self- Defense)

Copyright: Ocala, Fl.
All rights reserved.
By John Marinelli
10/19/2022

Print ISBN: 978-1-0879-99302
eBook ISBN: 978-1-0880-01226

johnmarinelli@embarqmail.com
www.marinellichristiabook.com

PREFACE

The purpose of this book is to alert the reader on the dangers of evil forces lurking in the shadows in these last days.

Page content will include: Burglary Statistics, Possibilities, Self-Defense Tactics, Do's & Don'ts, God's Will in taking a life of an intruder, Preventative Measures, Fight or Flight, Concealed Carry, Family Instructions, Overcoming A Victim Mentality, and other emotional threats to good health.

"Shadows In the Light of a Pale Moon" was written specifically for the Christian community. However, non-Christian folks can benefit from the many tips, detailed statistics, and right way teaching relative to gun safety and self-defense.

Primary emphasis is placed upon use of deadly force, preventing home invasions and situational tactics.

TABLE OF CONTENTS

INTRODUCTION

Benny, my fictional character, became a victim of a burglary and began his journey towards self-defense and restoration. He must now find peace and safety from the fear and pain of a home invasion.

Our story begins with the police at Benny's residence investigating the break-in where shots were fired and a 15-year-old boy lay dead on his living room floor. Benny's wife Sarah, is weeping and crying out to God saying, "Why Lord?" "Why Lord?"

Police Captain Courageous begins asking Benny questions to ascertain what exactly happened.

CHAPTER ONE:

THE TERROR BY NIGHT

CAPTAIN COURAGEOUS BEGINS HIS INVESTIGATION. Mister Ackerman, tell us, in your own words, what happened here tonight. I will need to establish a time line showing every action so please be detailed.

Benny begins…"My wife, Sarah and I had just retired for the night. She turned off all the lights and I checked all the doors to be sure they were locked. We just moved here from The Bronx, NY. We had to be sure the house was secured there because of the rising crime. We never thought that sort of thing would happen here.

Captain Courageous…So you retired for the night, then what happened?

Sarah responds…We heard a noise in the garage and then the door opened.

Benny interrupts…That door needed to be oiled. It squeaks when you open it. That's how we knew it was the garage door.

Benny continues…I told Sarah to dial 911 and let them know we have a burglar in the house. Then I reached for my 9-mil. pistol. I keep it in my top dresser drawer under my socks. I racked it and told Sarah to hide in the bedroom closet while I looked around.

Captain Courageous…Why didn't you wait for the police?

Benny…I had someone in my house looking to steal my stuff. I didn't know what other intentions he might have. All I knew at the time was, our lives could be in grave danger. I had to protect my family.

Captain Courageous…Family?

Benny…Yes family. We have two beautiful dogs and a singing bird that sometimes barks like the dogs. So, I peaked into the living room and saw three individuals. They were shadows in the light of a pale moon shinning into the living room. One had a baseball bat, one with a switch-blade knife and one with a gun. I yelled at them, telling them to get out of my house or I'll start shooting.

Captain Courageous…what happened then, Mister Ackerman?

Benny…I turned the light on and saw a man swinging a bat. He hit my lamp and broke my wife's favorite picture. I fired my gun into the ceiling as a warning but that didn't scare them off. Then the one with the gun fired at me. The bullet came so close that I could feel the rush of the wind it generated as it grazed my head. I fired back and the burglar fell to the ground.

Sarah…Tell him about the knife.

Benny…Oh yeah, the knife. I pulled the knife out of my shoulder as I fell to the floor. I did get off two more shots at the intruders but I don't think I hit them. They ran as I pulled the trigger.

Captain Courageous…What about your dogs?

Benny…They were closed up in the bedroom with my wife. But the bird was barking like the dogs the entire time. Between two dogs in the bedroom and one bird in the living room, all barking, it was really confusing.

Captain Courageous…Tell me again about how you shot the burglar.

Benny…I was terrified. I saw a man with a gun pointed at me and he was screaming, "Get down on the floor." I didn't have my glasses on and I don't see very well without them. All I really saw was one guy and it looked like he was about to shoot me. I raised my pistol and fired. I read in a magazine about, "Point and Shoot" and I did that.

Lieutenant Brooks…Captain sir, we caught the other two burglars, one was wounded and the other still had the baseball bat. The coroner examined the third and pronounced him deceased. There is a crowd gathering of neighbors. They all want to know what happened.

Captain Courageous…It's 2:30 AM. Doesn't anybody sleep in this neighborhood?

Lt. Brooks…Well, the TV channel 9 reporter is outside too and she is asking to talk to the homeowner.

Captain Courageous…That's not going to happen. Send them all away. This is official police business…and get those three squad cars back on patrol. This is not the police parking lot.

Sarah…The phone has been ringing ever since my 911 call for help.

Captain Courageous …Let me get this straight. Three burglars broke into your home. You turned on the lights, told them to leave and they attacked you with a baseball bat, knife and a 22 mil. gun. You fired three shots, one into the chest of the gun holder and two at the others as they were running away.

Benny…that is almost correct. But the two other shots were only after they threw a knife at me. Also, I shot one more time into the ceiling at the beginning as a warning.

Now what happens?

Captain Courageous….I have the 9 mil. pistol, you used to shoot the teenage burglar. Now I need all the rest of the guns and rifles you own. We can't let you keep deadly weapons until a hearing is conducted and a judge rules on the matter.

Benny…What about my 2nd amendment rights to own and bear arms? I have a right to own as many guns as I deem necessary. I will not give up my collection of pistols because I used one of them to protect myself and family.

Captain Courageous…You'll get them back if the court says it's ok. I either take your weapons or I take you to jail, come back with a court order to search your home and seize them.

Benny…Look, you are treating me as if I were the one at fault when in fact, the three burglars forcibly entered my home and threatened my life.

Lt. Brooks…That's just how it works. We have to follow the law. If you are a law-abiding citizen, you will comply.

Benny…ok, take the rest of the weapons but I better get them all back.

Captain Courageous…Here's what happens next. I will file my report. You will be able to get a complete copy in 2-3 days. Then a court date will be set to review this case to determine if you are mentally capable of owning these types of weapons.

Benny…And what do I use to defend myself if or when the two other burglars want revenge and come after me?

Lt. Brooks…You call 911 and we will come running.

Benny…Right!

CHAPTER TWO:

BENNY'S PRAYER

Benny…Dear Lord, I am so sorry for taking the life of that teenage burglar. I tried to shoot low to hit his legs but the pistol had such a kick that I ended up hitting him in the chest. I wasn't trying to kill him. What do I do now?

Sarah…Are you praying? You haven't done that in years. What are you praying about? Is it that boy you shot? If it is, don't worry about it. He had a gun and would have killed you and me if you didn't shoot.

Benny…You don't understand. The kid is dead and I am to blame. You know the scripture, "Thou shalt not kill." I never read any exceptions to the rule. There were other options but things happened so fast. I hardly had time to think. I was worried about the dogs and the bird and of course you. We could have just stayed in the bedroom and waited for the police.

Sarah…Do you think that God is mad at you for protecting us? Is his love and acceptance based upon how we obey the 10-commandments? You weren't looking to kill anyone. The intent of your heart was not that at all and God looks at the intent of the heart.

Benny…I need to talk to the paster of our church. It's a Bible based church and he will know what the Bible says. Maybe I can get some answers.

Pastor Jefferies…Hi Benny, I am sorry I missed your call the other day. What can I do for you?

Benny…I guess you heard about the shooting I was involved in last week. I need your help to sort it all out.

Pastor Jefferies…What exactly is bothering you about that night?

Benny…I shot and killed an intruder. He is dead and I am at fault. It's my fault that he is dead. The kid will never grow up, get married, have kids of his own. He is dead. That weighs heavy on my heart.

Pastor…Are you looking for me to absolve you from the guilt? Would you feel better if I were to say, "It's ok. Don't worry about it." I can not give you that, but what I can do is show you what the Bible says. Listen to what the dictionary and the Bible says about what constitutes a murder.

Dictionary term…The unlawful premeditated killing of one human being by another without justification or valid excuse. The meaning of MURDER is *the crime of unlawfully killing a person especially with malice and forethought.*

Biblical Term…The prohibition against murder is found in the Ten Commandments, the heart of Hebrew law (Exodus 20:13; Deuteronomy 5:17). Murder is the unlawful killing of a human being by another. Deliberately taking the life of a human being usurps the authority that belongs to God. The prohibition against murder is a hedge to protect human dignity.

Notice that both terms talk of "Willful Premeditation." It also points to the victim as being innocent. Your burglars were deliberately and actively engaged in an unlawful act that was planned out ahead of time. You did not seek them out to kill them. They sought you out to rob you and possibly kill you if you resisted.

There is another thing you need to consider and that is "Free Will" God has given every human being a free will to plan and do whatever comes to mind. He has also said that every action will be judged.

The Bible also says that every action is like a seed that if planted, will grow into a harvest whether good or bad. Evil will produce evil and good will produce good. Those burglars were planting seed of evil that grew up into a harvest and fell back upon them.

God does not look at the death of your teen burglar as murder. He instead sees it as a harvest that was growing up inside of that boy from the thoughts and actions he chose in life.

Today's world is much different than when our grandparents lived. They didn't even have to lock their doors at night. Now, we not only lock them but we have elaborate alarm systems to let us know when someone is lurking outside our windows.

Self-defense is a valid honorable reaction to an attack by evil forces. The Bible says a lot about self-defense. Here is one such passage.

The proper use of self-defense has to do with wisdom, understanding, and tact. In Luke 22:36, Jesus tells his remaining disciples, "If you don't have a sword, sell your cloak and buy one." Jesus knew that now was the time when his followers would be threatened, and he upheld their right to self-defense.

Just a short time later, Jesus is arrested, and Peter takes a sword and cuts off someone's ear. Jesus rebukes Peter for that act (verses 49–51). Why? In his zeal to defend the Lord, Peter was standing in the way of God's will. Jesus had told his disciples multiple times that he must be arrested, put on trial, and die (e.g., Matthew 17:22–23). In other words, Peter acted unwisely in that situation. We must have wisdom regarding when to fight and when not to. (Excerpt from Gotquestions.com)

My suggestion would be to seek the Lord about this matter and settle it in your heart that you were justified in what you did. Then maybe look into how you can help the family of the boy that died.

Lt Brooks…The court will rule on whether you were justified or not. The judge will ask you if you had to do it all over again were there any other choices you could have made and if so, why didn't you select one of them instead of the one you chose.

Benny…I was in fear of my life. It was the only thing I could do to save myself and my family.

Lt. Brooks…Not so, mister Ackerman. There are always other choices. I can think of two off the top of my head. Flee, get out of harm's way; Hide in a pre-designated room that locks until help arrives. I know that you could not flee but why didn't you hide and wait for the police to respond to your 911 call?

Benny…I have the right to stand my ground and defend myself from intruders. That's why I fought back…because I could.

Lt. Brooks…Having the right and doing the right thing are two different things. Yes, you have the right but how you stand your ground can make all the difference in how things turn out.

If you had locked yourself in your bedroom and waited for the police, the burglars could have just looked around and ran or the police could have captured them while you were safe and sound. Firing your pistol should have been a last resort.

Benny…You say I should have hidden from the burglars. How could I know before time that they would not break down the locked door?

Lt. Brooks…You could not have known but you could have waited until they began to break down the door before shooting. It's a wonder you are not dead.

Benny…why do you say that?

Lt. Brooks…First thing you did wrong was to leave the bedroom. You let the intruders know your exact position. Second, you turned on the lights further revealing your location. Third, you yelled at them to leave or you will shoot. You most likely made them mad and more willing to engage in violence. Finally, you allowed yourself to become a target for the shooter, the knife thrower and beaten with a baseball bat. You were lucky that they were just kids. A professional burglar would have taken you out right away.

One more thing: Now you are open to revenge from the other two burglars and/or the dead boy's family and friends. The sad thing is, this could have been avoided.

Sarah…We'll have to sell the house and move away. We can live with my sister in North Carolina until we get settled. We can't stay here anymore.

Captain Courageous…Leave them alone Brooks. Most folks are too distraught to take revenge. You don't have to run away. Things will settle down and your life will get back to normal.

CHAPTER THREE:

HERE COMES THE JUDGE

SARAH…ARE YOU OK BENNY? WE are supposed to appear before Judge Sanders in a few minutes. Let's take our seats.

Benny…Yeah, this is the hearing that Captain Courageous spoke of. I guess they will send me to jail or something for defending myself. I rehearsed every moment of that night so I have it clear. I even wrote a summary of that day.

Bailiff…Everybody rise for the honorable Lilly Sanders, Judge of the 5th circuit court in the state of Florida.

Judge Sanders…please be seated. We are here this morning to conduct a special hearing into the events of September 14th, 2022 and to determine the justification for using deadly force by mister Benny Ackerman.

Please be advised, this is not a criminal trial. It is, as I have stated, a hearing to determine if further action is necessary. This case was referred to me by the district attorney.

Mister Ackerman, tell the court, in your own words, what happened in the early morning hours of September 14th.

Benny…I would like to submit this written statement to the court. I wrote it all down so I wouldn't forget. And now, I will tell you what happened.

I was awakened by my dogs barking around 2:00AM. At first, I didn't think much of it because they often bark when they hear another dog or some other animal passing by. But then I heard my garage door begin to open, I became concerned. I knew it was that door because it squeaks when opened. It's the only door that squeaks. At that point I knew that there was an intruder.

I woke my wife, Sarah, and told her to call 911. Then I reached into my top dresser draw and grabbed my 9-mil. Pistol. I racked it, took off the safety and proceeded to investigate.

I yelled into the living room saying that I had a loaded gun and whoever is there better leave immediately. When there was no response, I fired a round into the ceiling as a warning shot. I figured that if I fired my gun whoever was there would know that I was serious. I could fix the ceiling and by shooting avoid any further trouble.

The room was pitch black and everything was quiet. Even the dogs were quiet. At that point, I thought the intruder had fled the scene so I turned on the light to have a look see.

It was then that I saw three young men, one with a baseball bat; one with a switchblade knife; and the 3rd had a gun in his hand. The gunman fired a shot at me from about 15 yards away. The bullet whizzed by me and went into the wall. I raised my pistol and fired back in a, "Point & Shoot" manner. I did not even aim, just pointed and fired. The gunman fell to the floor.

Judge Sanders…what happened then?

Benny…The other two ran but not before trashing my home. The baseball bat was swinging as the intruder ran. A switchblade knife was thrown at me and entered my right shoulder. I was in fear of my life and that of my family. I guess I am lucky to be alive.

Judge Sanders…Does anyone else want to add a comment or statement to mister Ackerman's story?

I have reviewed the police reports, witness statements and mister Ackerman's story that was submitted the day of the home invasion. I have also listened very carefully to his remarks today.

I see no cause to escalate this to a crime. Our state supports a "Stand Your Ground" course of action. However, I do see multiple flaws in mister Ackerman's actions. Therefore, it is my judgment and subsequent decree that mister Ackerman attend a court sponsored gun safety and self-defense class and that his weapons not be released to him until he has successfully graduated.

This court is adjourned.

CHAPTER FOUR:

AN OUNCE OF PREVENTION AND A
POUND OF INTELLIGENCE

O K EVERYBODY, MY NAME IS Professor Evans. I have been assigned to this group to teach the basics of good self-defense and gun safety. I do not mean hand-to-hand combat. My teaching expertise is in preventing a home invasion. To do that, you need to think like a burglar. So, tonight, we will think like a burglar and see where it takes us. But first I want to talk about Gun Safety.

Gun safety begins with an inspection of your home. Do all your windows lock? Do you have a "Dead Bolt" on your front door? Do you have a "Belly Button" or a wooden jam to keep your sliding glass doors from being opened easily? Do you have an alarm system? Securing your home will keep your family safe and your guns from easily being stolen.

The next consideration in basic gun safety is to know all about your weapon; how it works, how to load and unload it, how to dissemble and reassemble it, how to clean it, how to clear malfunctions and how to store it safely.

Finally, gun safety is all about keeping the weapons out of the reach of small children and teens that have not been educated in gun safety.

If you have not done these basic steps, you will most likely become a victim of a home invasion. That said, lets think like a seasoned burglar.

1. Would a burglar prefer breaking into a home during the daytime when no one is home or at night when the home is occupied?

2. Will a burglar pass on by or enter a home that is monitored by a burglar alarm company that displays it's sign in the yard?

3. Who is most likely to be attacked, ages 19-35 or senior citizens?

Seniors are less likely to be a victim. Daytime is better to break into a home and yes most burglars will pass on by when they see a sign from an alarm company.

Now, who can think like a burglar?

Thoughts of A Burglar

If you could listen in on the thoughts of an intruder, here's some of what he might be thinking:

1. OK, they left this window unlatched. It's an easy access.

2. Good, there are no dogs. I don't want to get bit.

3. Great, the front door is not a solid door. I can kick it down easily.

4. Darn, they have an alarm. Maybe they forgot to arm it.

5. Humm, newspapers building up, must be away…good target.

6. This house has high bushes; I can hide there if I need to.

7. Hey, no blinds or curtains. I can see into this house and what's inside.

8. I hear the T.V. I can't break in now.

9. I wonder where the master bedroom is. That's where the jewelry is.

10. Maybe the front door is unlocked. It was at the last place I robbed.

Knowing some of what an intruder thinks will help you devise a plan to secure your dwelling. Speaking of a plan, here's what Wiki says about deterrents.

Class participant Susan…I am supposed to remember all of this?

Professor…You bet. If you want to be prepared, you need to digest it all and keep my hand-outs as a referral library. Now, let's talk about deterrents.

Burglar Deterrents That Work

1. **Visible Window & Door Locks…**Burglars get into your home via the door or window, so providing a first-line deterrent like visible (and sturdy) locks is a step toward security. Do not be frugal with your locks. Your local locksmith can recommend the strongest, best locks for your home.

2. **Lock Your Doors**…this is so, so simple but many people fail to lock their doors. Lock up every time you go out, obviously, but also keep the doors locked when you're home – and especially at night. If you like to leave screened doors and windows open on a nice day, no problem; there are good locks for sturdy screens, too. And speaking of locks, all doors should have deadbolts and patio/sliding doors need special anti-entry devices to prevent removal from their frames.

3. **Get A Home Security Check**…Your local police department likely offers an underutilized but invaluable public service: home security checks. Call your local officers in blue, and ask for them to come out. They'll walk the inside and outside of your home, and suggest areas for improvement.

4. **Install An Alarm…**A home alarm system is one of the top ways to deter burglars from targeting your home. Several different systems and extras are available, from a basic alarm siren to a fortress. Take the maximum protection you can afford. Make sure your alarm company has

a fast response time, and consider whether you want the police automatically notified of an alarm event.

5. **Install Security Cameras…**The best defense is a good offense. Put burglars on the defense by recording their every move. You'll need indoor and/or outdoor security cameras with night vision and a decent hard drive to record a few days' worth of video. If you can't afford the real thing, fake cameras can also work as a good deterrent; just make sure they're quality fakes and not cheap plastic that thieves will easily identify as dummies.

6. **Motion Activated Lights**…Illuminate shadowed part of your home and access points with motion-activated floodlights. That's right, floodlights. If a light flips on, you want a wide viewing area.

7. **Strong Doors** ….Nearly 70% of burglars enter your home through a door. Install thick, solid wood doors that will be hard to kick in. If your doors have a window, install a secondary floor lock, so that after breaking the door window, a burglar cannot reach down to unlock your door and waltz into your home. Install hidden bracing in the doorframe.

8. **Safe & Secure…**In the event that a thief does breach your perimeter security, have your most precious valuables and weapons safely secured in a fireproof safe. Bolt the safe to the floor; otherwise, a strong burglar could cart it out.

Susan…We have to do all that just to be protected?

Professor…A friend once told me, "Failing to plan is really planning to fail." Evil and crime increases when good people do nothing. Your risk is greater when you ignore the issue.

Now, let's talk about what to do if you are caught in the middle of a home invasion. Listen up, Benny. You will see where you went wrong.

What To Do In A Home Invasion

(Excerpts from Wiki, how to do anything)

1. Avoid Searching For An Intruder.

We've all seen movies where the homeowner grabs a bat and sneaks through the house searching for an intruder. It's best, though, to avoid confrontation with the intruder if at all possible. An intruder can react violently, so instead of searching for the intruder, you should first try to escape or hide.

2. Come up with a simple code word that your family will recognize in an emergency.

If you need to warn your family members about an invasion, it's a great idea to have a code worked out in advance. You can shout this simple word or phrase, such as "ESCAPE!", to put them on the alert so that they can escape or run to a safe place.

3. Designate a safe room.

If you're not able to get out of the house, having a designated safe room (or even closet) can be a good idea. If at all possible, try to make your way to this safe room if you hear an intruder in your home.

4. Make sure your safe room locks from the inside.

Whether your safe room is your bedroom or a separate room in the house, you want to make sure that it has a solid door which locks from the inside and which can be quickly and easily barricaded. Consider installing a dead bolt on your bedroom door and/or the safe room for extra security.

5. Turn out the lights and remain as silent as possible.

You don't want to alert the intruder to your presence if at all possible, so make sure that all lights in the room are turned off.

6. Avoid calling out to the intruder.

You may be tempted to yell "We've called the police!" in order to make the intruder panic and leave as quickly as possible. This isn't a good idea because it will give away your hiding place. If, however, the intruder tries to break into the room where you're hiding, then it may actually be a good idea to yell "We've called police—they're on their way!". Use the plural "we" when you call out, even if you're alone. If the intruder thinks that there are more than one of you, he may panic and leave.

7. Call 911 as quickly as possible.

Once you are secure, call for help immediately. Be sure to provide the dispatcher with as many details as possible. For example, "My name is Sally Smith, and I live at 123 River Road. I hear two intruders in my home. I'm hiding in the upstairs back bedroom, and I think they are still downstairs in the living room." Try to keep the line with the dispatcher open so that they can listen in, provide you with updates on the progress of the police, and help keep you calm.

8. Choose your position in the safe room strategically.

If the intruder tries to break into the room where you are hiding, you're going to have to be prepared. Experts recommend that you stand in a corner that is on the opposite side of the door. Have your family members stand behind you. This way, if the intruder breaks into the room, you'll be able to see them before they see you, and you can quickly assess the situation to see if you need to fight (or shoot, if you are armed with a gun).

9. Remain in your safe room until the police arrive.

Even if you are sure that the intruder has left, it's best for you to stay put until the police arrive to secure your home. Continue to stay on the line with the emergency services dispatcher until you are told that the police have arrived **and** until the police announce themselves outside your door.

10. Make sure your entire house is checked by the police.

Especially if the suspect isn't caught. You should ask them to thoroughly check your house and property.

Susan…I'd probably be too afraid to do anything. I just won't remember.

Professor…Then be sure to write down all that you need to do and put it in a safe place where you can retrieve it if or when you need it.

I want to discuss using "Deadly Force" Your use of deadly force should be based upon the understanding that:

1. You are in grave danger and a serious threat of violence.

2. The intruder is in your home to Steal, Kill & Destroy.

3. The intruder has a deadly weapon of some
   kind. (Gun, Knife, Bat etc.)

4. The intruder will use deadly force to prevent capture.

5. Drugs are most likely being used and sought after.

6. The intruder is a burglar bent on doing evil.

Benny…So I was all wrong in the way I reacted the night they broke into my house. Is that right?

Professor Evans…I guess that is right. You did everything wrong. You searched for the intruders. You yelled at them, revealing your location. You turned on the lights so they could see exactly where you were. You left your wife alone and unprotected. You did not wait for the police to arrive and you fired your weapon into the ceiling as a warning telling the burglars that you were afraid and possibly an easy takedown. It's a miracle that you are alive.

CHAPTER FIVE:

ODDS AND POSSIBILITIES

P ROFESSOR…MISTER ACKERMAN WAS AN EXCEPTION to the rule. Let me share some statistics about home invasions.

You may be surprised to know that in America, 4 homes are invaded every minute, or about once every 15 seconds. Also, statistics show that if you live in the United States, you have about a 1 in 1000 chance of being robbed throughout a given year.

Sarah…That's a thousand to one. That is pretty good. There is no need to worry, right?

Professor…Tell that to Benny. He was the one in a thousand. Plus, 2.5 million homes each year also fall into that 1 in 1000 category.

Sarah…Yeah, but they were kids, not professional.

Professor…Most burglars are not professional. I think the professionals are ranked under 2%. Let's continue.

Burglars can get into your home in one of two ways. One is by entering through an unlocked door or window. In fact, over 30% of criminals don't have to do anything special to break into a home; they just waltz right in unrestricted, or hop through a window.

On the other hand, the other 60% of burglars use force to get into a home, by either breaking a window, or jimmying a weak knob lock.

Your front door is the way in which 33% of burglars gain access. This means, of course, that your front door is likely to be the main target of any kind of forced entry. As such, having a hollow front door is like an invitation to some burglars to kick the door down and barge right in.

Another interesting statistic is that 25% of burglars will attempt to disarm any kind of wiring they think is attached to your phone, or a home security system of some kind. If a burglar was to do something like this, we're talking about a pre-meditated act that puts you and your family at risk.

Once a burglar has robbed a home, they now know its weak points and can do so again at any time. Don't be one of those people who go through the ordeal of being robbed, only to be robbed yet again because they didn't change anything about the security level of their home.

If a robber has even attempted to break in and failed, your home's overall level of security should at least be analyzed in order to prevent future break-ins.

A recent Bureau of Justice Statistics Special Report tells us that in 28% of all burglaries, someone was home.

In addition, another upsetting statistic shows that 7% of people who were in the house at the time of the burglary had some form of violent crime committed upon them.

Considering there are around 2-million break-ins on average each year, 140,000 families are forced to face some sort of violent action. **(Statistics provided by "Your Home Security Watch")**

What does all these statistics tell us about the chances of us being a victim?

It says that your chances of being burglarized are 1,000 to 1 that you will become a victim. That is very small or should I say not much of a chance. Yes, it can happen like it did with the Ackerman's but the chances are really good that it will not happen to you.

It says that 72 % of all burglaries happen when no one is at home. The chances of a face-to-face encounter with a burglar is minimal.

As I conclude the segment of our course, I want to review the four laws of gun safety. You must learn them and know them in order to pass this class.

1. **The Gun Is Always Loaded.**

2. **Never Point The Gun At Something You Are Not Prepared To Destroy.**

3. **Always Be Sure of Your Target And What Is Behind It.**

4. **Keep Your Finger off The Trigger Until Your Sights Are On The Target.**

Are there any questions? Ok then, let's take a break and be back in a few.

Professor…Ok, let's continue our class instruction.

Class participant Bill…Aren't we at the end yet. I have other things to do.

Professor…You will stay until I am finished as the Judge said… and, you will not get your weapons back until I am satisfied that you are mentally responsible.

Now, listen up…Some states have self-defense laws. Florida, for example, has what's called "The Castle Doctrine."

The Castle Doctrine And "Stand Your Ground"

A Brief Summary

"Castle Doctrine" refers to the generally accepted common-law principle that one is not required to retreat when in one's own dwelling. Eliminating the requirement to retreat outside the home (i.e. in public) is generally referred to as a "Stand Your Ground" law.

As of October 1, 2005, Florida became a "No Duty to Retreat" (i.e. Stand Your Ground) state. The Florida Castle Doctrine law establishes that law-abiding residents and visitors may legally presume the threat of bodily harm or death from anyone who breaks into a residence or occupied vehicle and may use defensive force, including deadly force, against the intruder. With the passage of Florida's Stand Your Ground law, this principle now also applies in any other place where a person "has a right to be."

Essentially, that person has "no duty to retreat" if attacked and may "meet force with force, including deadly force if he or she reasonably believes it is necessary to do so to prevent death or great bodily harm to himself or herself or another or to prevent the commission of a "forcible felony". However, all of the generally accepted common-law principles of self-defense must still be followed.

The best Self-Defense Tactic is to avoid conflict and *Stay Out of Harm's Way.*

Benny…that's why I stood up and defended myself, because I could by law.

Professor…But Benny, you did it all wrong. That's why you are here now in this class…to learn the right way to stand your ground.

How many know what, "Street Smarts" means?

Bill…Isn't it to know the layout of a city and be able to find your way around?

Susan…I can tell you didn't grow up in New York. It means that you are aware of what is going on around you?

Professor…Susan is correct. It is commonly known as "Situational Awareness."

The key to your personal protection is being "Street Smart". It is the key to good self-defense. You always know what's happening around you. As you practice this perspective, you will observe the following:

1. Lots of folks are totally unaware of their surroundings.
    If there were a terrorist close by or a robbery about
    to happen, they would not even have a clue. They are
    too busy talking on their cell phones or texting.

2. Some folks are aware of what's going on around
    them but have a, "So What" attitude. They do
    not look at life in terms of self-defense.

3. Other folks watch people all the time. They see the nuts
    and weirdoes lurking in the shadows but do not neces-
    sarily see it as a personal threat. It's just part of life.

4. The last group of folks is the situationally aware. They always
    see things in terms of self-defense. They are always on the
    lookout for danger. If they see a strange man, they avoid him. If
    they see a conflict of any kind, they stay out of it, if at all pos-
    sible. They look for ways to escape instead of reasons to engage.

Should you decide to carry a loaded firearm, know that it is not meant to give you power. It is not supposed to give you a sense of egocentric euphoria. What it does do is provide an opportunity to protect your family and you.

Carrying the weapon concealed or openly, does us no good at all unless we are thinking like the bad guy and planning ahead with counter measures that are designed to keep us safe. This takes forethought and even thinking on the fly as situations arise.

Benny…That's a bit much, don't you think? I'll never have fun if I am always trying to determine who is or who is not an enemy.

Professor…You don't have to be absorbed with it so it consumes you. You do have to just be aware of what is going on around you. If you see a weird guy or a group that looks like a gang, you just go the other way. That's being "Street Smart."

Here's a question for you… ***When the shooting starts, what will you do?***

Class participant Tom…. You run and hide.

Susan…You stand your ground.

Bill……You go to a safe place.

Benny…You shoot back.

Professor…You are all right and you are all wrong. The answer should be obvious by now. ***It depends***… upon the environment you are in and what is really happening. Where is the nearest escape route? How many assailants are there? Can I get to cover quickly? Have the police been called? Can I get a clear shot?

Roll playing a situation out in different scenarios is a great strategy. It will help you stay alert and provide a plan of action if it ever happens. Most concealed carriers never think about what could happen and therefore have no self-defense strategy. In the time of trouble, they will not know what to do.

CHAPTER SIX:

DOING THINGS, THE RIGHT WAY

PROFESSOR…I WANT TO TALK NOW about, "The Value of Muscle Memory" Who can tell me what Muscle Memory is? Sarah…Isn't it the ability of your muscles to flex?

Professor…No, it is the ability to react without thinking. Most instructors will tell us that our handgun accuracy is a direct result of what is in our "Muscle Memory." Knowing what to do and how to do it is not enough. We must have it so ingrained in us that we do it without thinking. This is what muscle memory is all about.

If we have to think first, we will hesitate and that hesitation becomes a liability that could cause us to choke in a live combat situation with a home invader. Good handgun shooting is dependent upon you knowing what to do in any given situation and doing it without question.

Practice does not make perfect unless it is locked into your permanent memory. This requires repetition until you can do it all without thinking about it. I see this as riding a bike. When you 1st learn, you are thinking a lot but once you get it down, you do it automatically and never think about what you are doing. It's the same with shooting a handgun.

I read an article a while back about a study of the NYPD and their shooting accuracy in live situations. 77% missed their target from 2-7 yards away. The cause was because their target shooting was great but their muscle memory skills were not.

It must be second nature to you or it will not work to your advantage. Improving your accuracy can be done through *live firing*. Never dry fire your weapon. It is not good for the gun and does not help your accuracy.

Our form and technique in shooting must be correct. We need to learn it and then put it into our muscle memory so it is an automatic response in a crisis situation.

Remember, *muscle memory* is developed by repetition, doing it the correct way, over and over again until you can do it without thinking. Most gun owners fail in those critical moments of self-defense because they do not have *the right mindset*.

Let's take a short break and when we come back, we will look at Self-defense and Deadly Force.

Professor….Ok class, gather around. It's time to look at deadly force.

Educating yourself is the key to a proper mindset. This requires asking yourself the hard questions and working through them until you formulate answers that you can live with.

Here are a few hard questions that develop a proper mindset to carry a weapon for self-defense.

1. Will you actually shoot another person, a person that may or may not have a weapon? Self-defense could result in taking another's life to save yours.

2. Are you ready to carry a concealed weapon on your person…to the grocery store, to go bowling, to the movies, on a date night out or to dinner at a restaurant? Everywhere the law allows?

3. Are you ready to eat and breath self-defense so you can get it in your muscle memory? That will take Practice! Practice! and More Practice!

4. Are you prepared to be on the lookout for a terrorist everywhere you go? With all the random shootings in so many different

places, it is vital to become and stay aware of your surroundings. It could save your life and the life of your family.

5.   Are you willing to study and learn the lingo, the tactics and the techniques associated with self-defense? You will have to put in lots of hours to develop a perspective.

Self-defense in today's world could be a violent encounter with another human being that is bent on taking your stuff. These folks do not care about you. They steal for money to buy drugs or just for the fun of it. They survive at your expense. Some carry guns and some do not. You are allowed, by law, to use deadly force if necessary to defend yourself and your home.

Benny....We have some questions.

Professor...There six people in this class. Anyone can ask a question. Now go-ahead Benny, ask away.

Benny...What laws do we need to know that apply to the use of Handguns?

Professor.... There are special laws that apply anytime anyone uses deadly force, whether or not the weapon is concealed. Florida law defines deadly force as force that is likely to cause death or serious bodily harm. When you carry a handgun, you possess a weapon of deadly force. The law considers even an unloaded gun to be a deadly weapon when it is pointed at someone.

Benny...What about if I use my handgun to protect myself, like I did on September 14th?

Professor... Every state is different. Florida law justifies use of deadly force when you are:

1.   Trying to protect yourself or another person from death or serious bodily harm.

2.   Trying to prevent a forcible felony, such as rape, robbery, burglary or kidnapping.

Using or displaying a handgun in any other circumstances could result in your conviction for crimes such as improper exhibition of a firearm, manslaughter, or worse.

However, the kind of attack that will not justify defending yourself with deadly force is pictured in the following story:

Two neighbors got into a fight, and one of them tried to hit the other by swinging a garden hose. The neighbor who was being attacked with the hose shot the other in the chest. The court upheld his conviction for aggravated battery with a firearm, because an attack with a garden hose is not the kind of violent assault that justifies responding with deadly force.

Class Participant, Phil…What if someone uses threatening language so that I am afraid for my life or safety?

Professor…. Verbal threats are not enough to justify the use of deadly force. There must be an overt act by the person that indicates that he immediately intends to carry out the threat. The person threatened must reasonably believe that he will be killed or suffer serious bodily harm if he does not immediately stop his adversary.

Susan…What if someone is attacking me in my own home?

Professor… We talked about this earlier. Some states, including Florida have created an exception to the duty to retreat called the "Castle Doctrine." Under the castle doctrine, you need not retreat from your own home to avoid using deadly force against an assailant. The castle doctrine applies if an intruder attacks you in your own home. States that have this type of law report an 11% increase in gun related deaths. It shows us that more folks are defending themselves than before.

Tom…What if I am in my place of business and someone comes in to rob me? Do I have to retreat or can I defend myself and employees with deadly force?

Professor… The castle doctrine also applies when you are in your place of business. If you are in danger of death or great bodily harm or you are trying to prevent a forcible felony, you do not have to retreat. You can use deadly force in self-defense.

Benny…What if I point my handgun at someone but don't use it?

Professor… Never display a handgun to gain "leverage" in an argument. Threatening someone verbally while possessing a handgun, even licensed, will land you in jail for three years. Even if the gun is broken or you don't have bullets, you will receive the mandatory three-year sentence if convicted. The law does not allow any possibility of getting out of jail early.

Bill…When can I use deadly force in the defense of another person, like my neighbor or girl friend?

Professor… If you see someone who is being attacked, you can use deadly force to defend him/her if the circumstances would justify that person's use of deadly force in his/her own defense. In other words, you "stand in the shoes" of the person being attacked.

A person is justified in using or threatening to use deadly force if he or she reasonably believes that using or threatening to use such force is necessary to prevent imminent death or great bodily harm to himself or herself or another or to prevent the imminent commission of a forcible felony.

"Forcible Felony" means treason; murder; manslaughter; sexual battery; carjacking; home-invasion robbery; burglary; arson; kidnapping; aggravated assault; aggravated battery; aggravated stalking; aircraft piracy; unlawful throwing, placing, or discharging of a destructive device or bomb.

Class Participant, Janet…What if I see a crime being committed?

Professor…. A license to carry a concealed weapon does not make you a free-lance policeman. But, as stated earlier, deadly force is justified if you are trying to prevent the imminent commission of a forcible felony.

The use of deadly force must be absolutely necessary to prevent the crime. Also, if the criminal runs away, you cannot use deadly force to stop him, because you would no longer be "preventing" a crime. If use of deadly force is not necessary, or you use deadly force after the crime has stopped, you could be convicted of manslaughter.

Ok, let's move on in our search for truth and commonsense.

Tom…Wait a minute. I am a Christian and I have issues with gun control and killing of any kind.

Benny…We are also Christians and I do not have any problems with owning and carrying a gun for self-defense. It's my 2nd amendment right.

Professor…Ok, let's take a few minutes and look at the Christian perspective on gun control and the use of deadly force.

CHAPTER SEVEN:

THE CHRISTIAN PERSPECTIVE

PROFESSOR…SOME OF YOU KNOW THAT I am also a Christian. For me, that demands a higher view of life and death that establishes a mindset that is based upon Godly principles. Even if you are not a Christian, you have a moral obligation to seek out and apply honorable values.

Here's a question for all of you. "How Should A Christian View Gun Control?" Check out these stats on gun violence from GVA for 2022.

- Total number of gun violence death in 2022 (All Causes) 37,421
- Homicides, Murder, and Unintentional 17,141
- Suicide 20,328
- Mass shooting 581
- Mass murders 31
- Unintentional shootings 1,342

In 2020, 54% of all gun-related deaths in the U.S. were suicides, while 43% were murders, according to the CDC. The remaining gun deaths that year were unintentional, involved law enforcement or had undetermined circumstances.

Gun deaths in 2020 were by far the most on record, representing a 14% increase from the year before, a 25% increase from five years earlier and a 43% increase from a decade prior. There are more gun related deaths of women too. 57 women die every day as a result of gun violence. That's around 11,000 per year.

It sure seems to me that gun violence is getting worse and we need to be on guard at all times so we do not become one of the death by gun violence statistics.

I found this on the Internet as I prepared for this class. It comes to us from *Got/Questions.com*. Listen to what it says.

"The recent shootings across the United States have caused much heartache. The senseless and tragic incidents have also renewed the intensity of discussion regarding American gun laws. Politicians, sportsmen, and theologians have all weighed in on the issue of gun control. Guns are readily available in the U.S. and ownership is protected by the Constitution. How should a Christian support gun control? What does the Bible have to say?

The Bible was written long before the invention of any type of gun, so the phrase "gun control" will not be found in Scripture. However, the Bible records many accounts of wars, battles, and the use of weapons. Warfare is presented as an inevitable part of living in a fallen sinful world (Mark 13:7; James 4:1), and weaponry is a necessary part of warfare.

Weapons in the Bible were also used for personal protection. In some parts of Israel, robbers were common (see Luke 10:30), and many people carried weapons when they traveled. Carrying a weapon for self-defense is never condemned in the Bible. In fact, Jesus Himself mentioned it in a positive light on one occasion (Luke 22:35-38).

Christians are called to submit to governing authorities, and they are to obey the laws of the land (Romans 13:1-7; 1 Peter 2:13-17). This would have to apply to gun laws, too. If American gun laws change for the worst, American Christians should submit to them and work through a non-violent democratic means toward any desired alternatives. (That's why Christians should vote…to be sure our leaders are pro 2nd amendment.)

The Bible does not forbid the possession of weapons, and neither does it command such possession. Laws may come and go, but the goal of the believer in Jesus Christ remains the same: to glorify the Lord (1 Corinthians 10:31).

Another Biblical principle to consider is that "all who live by the sword will die by the sword" (Matthew 26:52). Jesus said this to Peter when Peter tried to mount an imprudent "defense" of Jesus against the mob that had come to arrest him.

Peter's actions were not only futile against such a "large crowd armed with swords and clubs" (verse 47), but his rash behavior also belied Jesus' submissive attitude (verse 50) and worked against the fulfillment of Scripture (verse 54). There is "a time for war and a time for peace" (Ecclesiastes 3:8), and Peter confused the two.

Christianity supports personal freedom. Romans 14:1-4 indicates that, when Scripture does not clearly address a particular issue, there is freedom for individual choice. America has historically embraced the concept of personal freedom that resonates with this principle, and the founding documents, (2nd Amendment), guarantee wide freedoms regarding firearms.

Some point to Matthew 5:9, in which Jesus pronounces a blessing on the peacemakers, and apply it to the issue of gun control. The idea is that guns are antithetical to peace. This may be more of a philosophical or political idea than a theological one, however. There is nothing theologically, or even logically, that links guns to a lack of peace; sometimes, guns help maintain civil peace.

Debates over whether to control guns or how much to control them depend largely on political and philosophical arguments, not moral ones. This is not to say that there is no moral component to the issue. Obviously, the gun itself is amoral, an object that can be used for good or for evil. More important is the morality of the person wielding the gun, and that is too often the missing consideration in the gun control argument.

The fact that some sinners use guns to commit sin does not mean guns are the problem. Sin is the problem, and that's a moral and spiritual issue. Since the very beginning of humanity, people have been killing other people, with and without weapons (see Genesis 4). Taking a certain weapon out of circulation might make murder more difficult but by no means impossible.

As far as the Bible is concerned, the use of guns is a matter of personal conviction. There is nothing unspiritual about owning a gun or knowing how to use one. There is nothing wrong with protecting yourself or loved ones. We should seek to neutralize threats without violence whenever possible. However, we need to also be ready to stand up to any evil threat and protect what is ours…See I Peter 5:8. It says, in so many words, that we are to resist the devil and he will flee from us.

!!! Remember !!! Your Greatest Defense Is God

Psalm 34:7 tells us…"The angel of the LORD encamps all around those who fear Him, And delivers them." NKJV

To fear the Lord is to reverence Him in all that you do. Do this & God's angel will set up his camp of "Warring Angels" all around you, to protect you and even deliver you from harm.

As a Christian who carries a concealed weapon, I believe that the best course of action is to not be where there is violence or the threat of bodily harm. I look for ways to stay out of harm's way.

If you see two people fighting, don't get involved. Instead, call 911. If danger comes knocking at your door, go next door if possible and call the police. You should use deadly force only as a last resort. If you see a suspicious person in your neighborhood, call 911.

If I were in a store and it is being robbed, I'd hide and call 911. I will not get involved unless there is a threat of violence or a loss of life.

However, I will not act unless I am in a good shooting position and have a clear shot.

I figure that me and my family comes first when it comes to self-defense. I can recall a time when a brother of a co-worker was in a bar when another man came in with a shotgun. He was after a guy at the end of the bar. The two men exchanged words and the dispute escalated.

The brother of my co-worker stood up and confronted the would-be shooter. The shooter said to get out of his way or he would blast him to kingdom come. The co-worker's brother said, "You haven't got the guts to pull the trigger" The would-be shooter did in fact pull the trigger and the co-worker's brother died that night. He made the fatal mistake of getting involved when he didn't have to. *(True Story)*

CHAPTER EIGHT:

"WHAT IF" SCENARIOS
(TAKEN FROM VARIOUS WEB SEARCHES)

PROFESSOR…LET'S LOOK AT SOME SITUATIONS and possible responses. There are many variables in any situation so an absolute for success will be hard to formulate. However, knowing ahead of time what could happen and some ways to protect yourself is better than facing the threat with no thought or knowledge at all. In all cases, it is understood that you have a concealed weapons license and access to a firearm during the encounters. The use of "Deadly Force" is now under consideration.

Situation #1….. Burglary

You are returning home from an outing. It is almost dark. You pull into your driveway, only to realize that your front door has been broken and is now open. You, as usual, are carrying concealed. **What do you do?**

Strategy… Stay in your vehicle and immediately call 911. You do not know if there are burglars still in your home or if they have come and gone. You do not know how many, if any, are inside. Let the police investigate and secure the property before you enter your home. Pulling your gun and rushing into an unknown situation could cost you your life.

Variables… The invader (s) come running out of your home as you pull up. What now? Using deadly force against fleeing thieves is not a good practice because they are already outside your home running away. There is no active threat to do bodily harm to you at this point. Let them go but take notes as to clothing, race, height and weight, direction of get-a-way, etc.

Remember, your well-being is worth more than your stuff. If he or they come out shooting or are running towards you, then there is a definite threat and deadly force is justified. However, facing armed thugs with your family in the car may not be the best scenario. It's ok to flee the scene to a safer location. Back out of your driveway and leave the area until the police arrive.

Situation #2… Parking Space Dispute

You are carrying concealed as you are doing errands and encounter an agitated man who is angry at the world and wants to take it out on anyone he encounters. He approaches you cursing at you because he thinks you took his parking space. ***What do you do?***

Strategy… Using deadly force to resolve an argument is not lawful. We don't shoot everyone that we disagree with. However, if the situation escalates into a threat to do bodily harm, you are justified to defend your-self with deadly force. If the man does not show a weapon, there may not be cause to use yours. Reasonable force can be applied. Sometimes, you can also just walk away from the conflict.

Your goal should be to de-escalate the situation by calming down the person who is angry. That may not be possible but an attempt is neces-sary before you use a weapon to resolve the matter. Your tone of voice should be calming and your speech should not be threatening in any way.

If all else fails, use the "Three Step Rule" that says take one step back as you try to resolve the situation calmly, being sure to speak loud enough to draw the attention of anyone around that could later be a witness.

Repeat this step back process two more times and then stand your ground. Tell him the police are on the way and he should leave. You have now made three attempts to calm the, "would-be" attacker and reduce the threat.

If this doesn't work, nothing will. Tell the man to keep his distance or you will use deadly force against him. You should have your gun drawn and racked by your side. If he moves into your space and has no weapon, reasonable force would apply, not deadly force.

If you see a weapon as he moves into your space, the threat has reached an immediate threat to do great bodily harm… shoot him.

Variable…Some would say, "Just turn and run" but that opens up the possibility of an attack from behind where you cannot see if he has a weapon or what. Standing your ground is the safest plan of action.

Dialing 911 is recommended as soon as you encounter the man. Just tell them that an angry man is about to attack you and where you are. Let them know you have a weapon and will use it to defend yourself, if necessary. This will put you at the top of their response list.

Be sure to tell the 911 operators what you are wearing and exactly where you are in the parking lot. Keep your phone on so the police can hear your conversation with the mad man. Tell the man that you have called 911 and he should leave you alone.

Your goal in this situation is to delay any attack until the police arrive. The 3-step attack strategy can help but it may all happen in a flash so be ready and mentally prepared to act. It's your life that hangs in the balance.

Situation #3… Home Invasion

You are a victim of a home invasion. Two teenage boys have broken into your home by breaking down the front door and are now rushing in to steal anything they can find. It's 2:30 am and the crash of the door being broken wakes you up or your alarm goes off. *What do you do?*

Strategy… Most burglaries take less than 2-3 minutes. They enter and run straight for jewelry, cash or electronics. They are in and out faster than most folks can react. You should have your guns close enough to get to in a hurry and loaded, (Armed and Ready). All family members should know exactly what to do. Set up family drills if necessary, so kids remember.

Call 911 as soon as possible then retreat to a "Safe Room". Weapons are loaded &/or racked. Do not turn on lights. It will give away your location. Close the door to the "Safe Room". It most likely will be your bedroom. Find a spot that offers the best coverage and gives you the advantage. Do not call out to the intruder(s). Wait for the police and keep that line open, talking to them every step of the way.

If they are still trying to enter your safe room, keep shooting until the threat is eliminated. Be sure to inform the 911 operators of what room you are in and that you have firearms. Should the door open, shoot immediately, even if it is through the door. Don't give the intruders an opportunity to see you. One or two shots will most likely cause them to flee.

Variables… The intruders have guns and shoot back at you. *Now what?* Be sure your location in the "Safe Room" is not in the direct line of fire from the door. Also, if you can, pull a dresser out and use it as a shield or hide behind something that will conceal your location.

If other family members cannot get to your designated "Safe Room," tell them to close the door of another room where they are and move a bed or dresser in front of the door so it is not easily accessible. Also, be sure 911 operators know about any changes to your plan. If any family member can flee to the outside and run for safety, do so as soon as possible.

Situation #4… C-Store Robbery

You stopped at a convenience store such as Race Track to get gas. A lone gunman is inside robbing the place. He runs out of the C- Store and across your line of sight. You are pumping gas and are carrying concealed. *What do you do?*

Strategy… Because the armed man is running away and to your knowledge, no individual has been harmed, let him run. Stay out of harm's way. Hide from his sight if possible so he does not see you as a threat. We are not called to be volunteer cops. We may be trained to shoot a gun but most of us know nothing about Law Enforcement. Leave it up to the professionals.

You can be a great witness to the crime by gathering vital info like height, weight, distinguishing marks, type of weapon, get-a-away car & direction etc. Don't try to be a hero.

Variable… The armed gunman is running from the C-Store straight for you. You are in the wrong place and cannot avoid an encounter with the armed man. His gun is in hand and he is waving it back and forth. *Now what do you do?*

Self-Defense is the first and only priority. The armed man is not just running away from the scene of a crime but has now involved you. You don't know if he wants your vehicle to use as a get-a-way car or you as a hostage or both. You do know that the threat is real and imminent.

SHOOT HIM… before he invades your space or shoots you. It's the only way to eliminate the threat. Do not delay. It takes about one and a half seconds to run 21 feet. He who hesitates is lost. However, there is an alternative action…*run like hell*. But be aware that the armed criminal may think that you took the keys with you and might start shooting at you as you run. It's better to take cover behind the wheel of your vehicle and shoot. You have a legal right to use deadly force to defend yourself.

Situation #5… Terrorist Attack

You are at an open-air concert with hundreds of other music lovers. Several shots are fired and people start running in every direction to get away from the shooter. ***What do you do?***

Strategy… Running aimlessly is not a good strategy. You do not know where the shooter is and if there is only one. One shooter could be shooting to cause people to run directly into the path of another shooter thereby causing a crossfire situation. It's better, if possible, to seek out cover and evaluate the situation. Run to the nearest structure or place of cover.

Hide until you can see a clear path to safety. Do not draw your weapon until you are ready to use it. You might be seen as the shooter.

Variable… There is no cover nearby and you are being pushed by the crowd in a certain direction as they run. ***Now what?*** If this happens, run with your eyes open, looking for people falling around you from being shot. Listen for single or rapid fire to determine type of weapons being used and try to measure distance and direction. If all else fails and people are being shot around you, fall down and play dead. The shooter will most likely seek upright targets, not stationery targets that he thinks are already dead. As you lay on the ground, be as still as possible and watch for the shooter in case he comes your way. Have your gun racked and ready.

If the threat has moved on towards the running crowd, maybe there is a chance to escape in the opposite direction. Watch for possible escape routes.

Situation #6… Defense of Others

You are in a fast-food restaurant when a shooter enters and begins to shoot people. ***What do you do?***

Strategy… A responsible gun owner that carries concealed will always scope out the establishment upon entering. He will look for exits and never sit with his back to an entrance. When people in the restaurant are in jeopardy, you have a duty to stand against the shooter before he kills everyone. You have just become their defense. However, that does not mean you stand up and call the shooter's attention to you. It is best to look for a location in the restaurant that gives you the shooting advantage. There may not be a shooting advantage location but then again there may be. Look for it and adjust. Then shoot the shooter and keep shooting until he is down and no longer a threat.

Variables… There is no tactical shooting advantage. You are in the open and in the line of fire. ***What next?*** Shoot immediately for center mass of the shooter at least three times. Then move to a different location quickly so the shooter has to adjust. Keep shooting and moving towards an exit and get out as fast as possible.

Note: Location evaluation is to know your surroundings. Are there guys with hoods, knapsacks or other possible give-a-ways as to their possible intent? Being aware is 90 % of the battle. The other 10% is muscle memory and training to know what to do if and when it happens.

Situation # 7…Road Rage

Road Rage has come to your doorstep. You are driving on the highway and inadvertently cut another driver off as you turn. That driver is furious and chases you down the road honking and screaming at you. He follows you until you stop at a light and then gets out of his car and walks towards your car. You are carrying concealed. ***What do you do?***

Strategy… The best thing is to just drive away and leave him standing in the street. If that is not possible, do not stay in your car. Step out so you can see what is around you and if the angry man has a weapon or not. A weapon can be a bat, a stick, a knife, or anything that could be used to inflict serious bodily harm.

Stay calm and try to de-escalate the situation by letting him vent. You can respond by saying you are sorry for cutting him off and it was not an intentional act of aggression. This is your best defense. It allows for talk instead of action.

Do not allow him to invade your space. Keep stepping away to create a "Safe Zone" between you and him. Be sure to repeat your apology several times. It's ok to be wrong, even if you are not. It is better to take the fault than to kill another human being. Sometimes a simple apology is enough.

Variables… The road rage man cannot be calmed. He insists on getting even by an act of violence. If and when you realize talking will not accomplish a satisfactory result, draw your weapon and be ready to use it. This decision can happen before you even begin a dialog with the angry man. Being ready is the key. Deadly force can be a choice that is later decided based upon the actions of your adversary. If you draw your weapon, do not show it. Keep it at your side or behind you until it is time.

The time to use deadly force is when the threat is imminent. There are signs like seeing that the man now has the opportunity and the ability to inflict serious bodily harm. You also honestly feel that your life is in grave danger.

Taking the 1st blow is not recommended. Remember the 3-step rule. Tell the man that you will use deadly force if he does not back off. However, be aware that you may not have enough time to say anything. You may have to shoot without any exchange of words. That depends on the actions of the other man.

Your self-defense is the priority. As long as you perceive that bodily harm is imminent and/or in the process of happening, you have the lawful right to fire your weapon. If you shoot, know that you are accountable for every bullet fired. That being said…keep firing until there is no longer a threat.

Unless you are a marksman, aim for center mass of the man's body. Do not focus on legs or head or arms. It is harder to hit unless you are a crack shot. Your goal should be to take the man down so he cannot harm you. However, this, "Deadly Force" action should be a last resort, used only when there is no other alternative.

Situation #8... Strangers Arguing

You are walking down the street to get some fresh air. You are carrying a concealed weapon as you always do. Suddenly you see two men arguing and about to get into a fight. *What do you do?*

Strategy... Getting involved in someone else's dispute could be bad for your health. You could end up being the target of their anger because you sought to stop their aggression towards each other.

The best action is to dial 911 and let the police handle the dispute. Then evaluate the situation to see if there are weapons being used in the fight. The only reason to get involved is to keep one from killing the other. If a firearm or knife is visible and about to be used against the other man, you can shout at them to stop and drop the weapons. Shooting the man that is armed may be the only way to save the unarmed man from being wounded or even killed.

Verifiable... Both men are armed and dangerous. *What then?* I suggest calling 911 to report the situation as you seek cover. Stay out of the fight and try to not be seen so one or both don't shoot at you.

You don't know if the two men are gang members, criminals or friends. The fact that both have guns and are about to use them on each other should tell you to keep out of sight and inform the police.

Do not participate in their gun battle. It's not you fight. However, if there is a survivor and he sees you, you may be in grave danger and then, only then, be prepared to defend yourself. Be sure to keep an open line to 911 so they know everything that you know.

Situation #9... Attempted Rape

Two men are dragging a screaming young girl into an alley where they intend on sexually assaulting her. *What do you do?*

Strategy… It is lawful to use deadly force to protect another human being from serious bodily harm. You may be the only one that can save the young girl from being raped. Call 911 immediately. Do not rush into the alleyway. Survey the area to be sure you know how many men are involved and their location in proximity to the young girl. You don't want any surprises. You can draw your weapon and fire a warning shot yelling at the men to leave the girl alone. This may be all that is necessary to scare off the attackers.

Take cover in case they have guns. In most cases, the men will run after hearing the 1st shot fired. Let them run. Do not chase after them because you could run right into a trap. Give detailed info to the police and let them capture the men.

Variables… The men are armed and shoot back at you. ***What should you do then?***

You are not a vigilante or volunteer cop. You are a responsible gun owner that is carrying a concealed firearm who just happened upon a crime being committed against a woman. Get out of the line of fire.

Stay connected to the 911 operators. Follow their instructions. Do not try to be a hero. The fact that you fired at the men, scaring them, will most likely stop the attempted rape.

You can still shoot again if necessary to keep them a bay but what you do not want is a gun battle. You will be outnumbered and most likely with less ammo than they have. Stay out of sight if possible and aware at all times until the police arrive.

Situation # 10… Robbery While Shopping

You are just leaving the grocery store and walking through the parking lot to your car. As you get close to your vehicle, you see a man out of the corner of your eye, coming towards you. He is wearing a hooded sweatshirt and has his hand in his pocket as though holding a gun. You are carrying a concealed firearm. ***What do you do?***

Strategy… Do not go to your car. Instead, head over towards where there are other people. Do not become isolated and alone. Go back into the store, if necessary, and call the manager to assist you in getting safely to your car. Report the suspicious men, however, realize that the man may just be a passerby and nothing more.

Variables… The suspicious man is in fact a bad guy and is looking to rob you. He has popped out of nowhere and is now 10 feet away from you as you unlock your door to load groceries. He says he has a gun and demands money. He is too close to run. ***What now?***

· If you can see him coming, you should have time to draw your weapon and have it racked. If he actually has caught you off guard and you have no time to react, you must assume that the man actually has a gun in his pocket, even though you cannot see it. However, he most likely, is not prepared to use it if he doesn't get his way. He is looking for a quick score, not a fight.

Do not challenge or threaten him. Instead, try to reason with him. You have a choice. Give him your money and hope he doesn't have a gun and runs away or stand your ground and fight to defend yourself.

If you decide to fight, try this…push him hard so he falls down and away from you. Pull your gun and shoot him as he scrambles to get back up. You will be reacting on the assumption that he has no gun. Let's hope you are right.

If you do not fight, the only other course of action is to give him your money and hope he doesn't shoot you. I'd rather stand my ground because most criminals are also cowards. When confronted, they run away. The choice is yours.

Situation # 11… Spouse Abuse

You and your spouse were arguing. Things get out of hand and end up in an all-out fight where your spouse attacks you with a baseball bat. After dodging the bat swings and running back and forth, you realize that your spouse's anger is way off the scale and you are in immanent serious danger. You know where the firearm is kept and can easily get to it. ***What do you do?***

Strategy… Do you really want to shoot your spouse? Anger is not a good thing and has often led to serious violent behavior that is regretted later. Sometimes, the best course of action is to run. Get out of the house and run away. This will give your spouse time to calm down. Walking or running away from a fight is better than killing or being killed in an angry stupor.

Variable… Your spouse has a history of abusive behavior. ***Now what?*** Call 911 and get the abusive behavior on record with your local police department. Get a restraining order to protect you against stalking and your spouse entering your dwelling. Maybe you should make arrangements to live elsewhere.

Demand marital counseling. Get your concealed weapon license and carry a firearm for self-defense. Take self-defense courses and if things do not progress, file for a divorce.

You do not need to kill as a result of a domestic dispute. However, you do have a right to protect yourself from serious bodily harm. Using deadly force is or should always be a last resort.

Situation # 12… Run, Hide, Fight

Professor…You will need to know four things about what to do when shots are fired.

The 1st is: Attack Recognition

Properly responding to danger actually begins well before the first shot is fired when people adopt a mindset that recognizes the world is a dangerous place and that they are ultimately responsible for their own safety.

Once a person understands the possibility of being targeted and decides to adopt an appropriate level of situational awareness, he or she will be mentally prepared to quickly realize that an attack is happening, something security professionals refer to as attack recognition.

The earlier a person recognizes that an attack is developing, the better chance he has to avoid it. But even once the attack has begun, a person can still keep it from being a successful one by quickly recognizing what is happening and getting away from the attack site by running or hiding — or fighting back if they cannot run or hide.

The 2nd is: Finding the Attack Site

However, once a person has recognized that an attack is taking place, a critical step must be taken before he can decide to run, hide or fight: He must determine where the gunfire or threat is coming from. Without doing so, the victim could run blindly from a position of relative safety into danger. I certainly encourage anyone under attack to leave the attack site and run away from the danger, but one must first ascertain if he is in the attack sight before taking action.

Many times, the source of the threat will be evident and will not take much time to locate. But sometimes, depending on the location — whether in a building or on the street — the sounds of gunfire can echo, and it may take a few seconds to determine the direction it is coming from. In such a scenario, it is prudent to quickly take cover until the direction of the threat can be located. In some instances, there may even be more than one gunman, which can complicate escape plans.

Fortunately, most active shooters are not well trained. They tend to be poor marksmen who lack experience with their weapons. During the July 2012 shooting in Aurora, Colorado, James Holmes managed to kill only 12 people — despite achieving almost total tactical surprise in a fully packed movie theater. That was because of a combination of poor marksmanship and his inability to clear a jam in his rifle.

This typical lack of marksmanship implies that most people killed in active shooter situations are shot at close range. Thus, it behooves potential victims to move quickly to put as much distance between themselves and the threat. Even the act of moving, especially if moving away at an angle, makes one a much harder target for a poorly trained marksman to hit.

The 3rd is: Concealment And Cover

It is also important to think about and distinguish between concealment and cover. Items that conceal, such as a bush, can hide you from the shooter's line of vision but will not protect you from bullets the way a substantial tree trunk will. Likewise, in an office setting, a typical drywall construction interior wall can provide concealment but not cover, meaning a shooter will still be able to fire through the walls and door. Still, if the shooter cannot see his or her target, they will be firing blindly rather than aiming their weapon, reducing the probability of hitting a target.

In any case, those hiding inside a room should attempt to find some sort of additional cover, such as a filing cabinet or heavy desk. It is always better to find cover than concealment, but even partial cover — something that will only deflect or fragment the projectiles — is preferable to no cover at all.

There are many examples from the Paris and Bamako armed assaults of people who ran away from the scene of the attacks and survived. In the Bamako attack there were also many people who barricaded themselves inside their hotel rooms and hid until the authorities could rescue them. The August 2015 incident aboard a Paris-bound train provided a good example of potential victims who were trapped aboard a train car and fought back to end an armed assault.

Some people have mocked the simplicity of run, hide, fight. But as these cases demonstrate, all three elements of this mantra can and do save lives.

The 4th is: Reasonable Force

The general principle is that the law allows only reasonable force to be used in the circumstances and, what is reasonable is to be judged in the light of the circumstances as the accused believed them to be (whether reasonably or not). In assessing whether a defendant had used only reasonable force, Lord Morris in *Palmer v R* [1971] AC 814, felt that a jury should be directed to look at the particular facts and circumstances of the case. His Lordship made the following points:

* A person who is being attacked should not be expected to "weigh and know the exact measure of his defensive action".

* If the jury thought that in the heat of the moment the defendant did what he honestly and instinctively thought was necessary then that would be strong evidence that only reasonable defensive action had been taken.

* A jury will be told that the defense of self-defense will only fail if the prosecution showed beyond reasonable doubt that what the accused did was not by way of self-defense. Self-defense laws restrict the protections of such a defense for those who initiate the conflict.

There are two ways a person can remain protected under self-defense laws if he was the one to start the conflict. The first is if he chose to leave the fight and informed the aggressor of his surrender, and the aggressor pursued him anyway. The second is if the other person responded to the presentation with aggressive force.

Benny…This class has been really helpful.
Sarah….That's for sure. Can we go home now?.

Tom…. .I don't know. There's too much to have to learn. I think I will just call the police and run away into the night.

Phil……I think it's been a real eye opener.

Susan… I think you all are crazy. There are just too many guns.

Bill…….We should get together next year at this same time and see who is still alive. lol

Professor…We are not finished. Here's a handout to take home. It's a sheet on the statistics of self-defense and burglaries. I will read it so I make sure you all know what it says.

CHAPTER NINE:

STATISTICAL ANALYSIS
THIS SURVEY WAS CONDUCTED IN 2020

In September of 2020, The Zebra conducted a nationwide survey of 1,500 American homeowners and renters to gain deeper insight into common concerns and oversights regarding personal security and safety. The survey found that:

- 46.9% of people don't have a home security system installed in their home.
- 20.2% of people have had their cars burglarized, while only 5.8% had their homes burglarized.
- 15.9% of respondents chose their dog for security reasons.
- External cameras were listed as the most important feature to have in a security system (32.3%). Motion sensors (28.6%) and floodlights (24.5%) were found to be in the top three most important features.
- 17.2% of people do not lock their front doors while at their home, despite the front door being the access point for 34% of burglars.
- 56.1% of respondents have not taken a personal safety training class.
- 55.4% of respondents have a fire safety evacuation plan.
- 38% of people own a weapon for personal safety reasons.

- 57.5% of women have taken a personal safety training course while only 42.5% claimed they had as well.
- 55.7% of women lock the front door while they're home, while only 44.3% of men do so. 61.1% of women post on social media when they are away from home, potentially alerting would-be burglaries of an easy target.
- Women listed a video doorbell as the most important feature in a security system. Men found that a digital door lock was most important.
- More men than women considered safety and security when purchasing a dog.
- More men than women own a weapon for personal safety.

For more information on yearly burglary crime rates, consider visiting the FBI's Criminal Justice Information Services Division.

- Early data in 2019 shows a drop of 3.1% in the number of burglaries and violent crimes for the first 6 months of 2019 when compared in 2018.
- More than 7% of homes fell victim to property crimes in 2018.
- In 2017, the FBI reported 1,401,840 burglaries with 57.5% of all burglaries involving forcible entry.
- A 2-year trend showed that the burglary rate dropped 1.3% in 2016 in comparison with the 2015 estimate.
- In 2015, Burglary crimes made up for 19.8% of all property crimes. Larceny and theft accounted for 71.4% and motor vehicle theft made up 8.9%.

These are old statistics now that we are living in 2022, and about to enter 2023. The crime rate in the United States is rising fast. It is even out of control due to open borders that caused a flood of illegal aliens to enter. With their arrival came more crime. Defunding the police in many large cities didn't help. The average citizen is forced to defend themselves. They can no longer depend on a skeleton police force.

Home invasion statistics by room

For further analysis, review the data sources for these statistics from the FBI, Bureau of Justice Statistics, and Statistica.

- 9% of burglars use the garage door as their access point.
- 22% of break-ins happen through the back door.
- 2% of burglars attempt to gain entrance through the second floor.
- 81% of home robberies begin on the first floor.
- 9% of burglars gain access in the basement.
- 23% of burglars enter a home through a window.

Statistics around when burglaries occur

According to Crimepreventiontips.com and the Jacksonville State University:

- Every 15 seconds a home burglary occurs in the United States. This means that approximately 4,800 burglaries happen every day.
- Break-ins occurring between 6 AM and 6 PM increase in likelihood by 6%.
- Most burglaries happen in the summertime between the summer months of June and August.
- Frequent home invasions happen between the hours of 10 am and 3 pm when the home owners are commonly away from the home.
- However, 27.6% of all home burglaries, someone is home during a burglary.

Property crime statistics

Analysis of FBI and the US Department of Justice data finds. Over 1 million burglaries are committed each year in the US:

- 66% of burglaries affect residential properties.
- 34% of the burglaries that happen each year affect small businesses.
- Over half (65%) of burglaries occur during daylight hours since that is when most people aren't home.
- All burglary victims lose an average of $2,416.
- In total, victims of burglaries (both private and public) lose an estimated $3.4 billion in personal property each year.

Criminal psychology statistics

The FBI's Uniform Crime Reporting (UCR) Program has identified the following data.

- After an arrest is made, 65.1% of people personally know their thief, meaning there's a very good chance your neighbor or acquaintance could attempt to rob you.
- Only 12% of all burglaries are planned in advance. Most thieves admit a break-in was an impulse decision.
- 95% of burglaries involve a forceful entry into the home, which means physical damage to your personal property.
- Over 60% of assaults, including the heinous crime of rape, happens during home invasions.
- Mapped areas of burglaries have determined that most burglars have been found to strike homes within a few miles of their residence.
- The average burglary lasts only 8 to 10 minutes.
- 44% of break-ins in the US happen in the South.

- There are around 100 burglaries that result in homicide every year in the United States
- In the US, about a third of home invasions are repeat burglaries.
- The typical burglar in 2018 was a white male aged 18 to 24.
- Only 30% of perpetrators were armed in the case of a home invasion.

A break-in occurs every 26 seconds in the US. This adds up to 2.5 million break-ins every year, with more than half of those burglaries occurring in homes.

Are you aware that you're eight times more likely to be involved in a home invasion attack than you are to be involved in a house fire?

Professor…Now each of you will take this self-help true or false test. Number your sheet from 1-35 and when I read the question put a "T" or an "F" by each number. I will give you the answer after each question. You can grade yourselves. Be honest…no cheating!

CHAPTER TEN:

A SELF HELP TRUE FALSE TEST
TAKEN FROM THE INTERNET ON 10/22/2022

1. A basic gun safety course is all that is needed to obtain a concealed carry license in the state of Florida.

_X_True __ False

2. Ongoing education is necessary for only those that want to be an instructor.

_x_True __False

3. A responsible gun owner is actually a, "Freelance Policeman" and should be ready at all times to defend others that may be in trouble.

__True _x_False

4. Some states tell us we can "Stand Our Ground" if and when we are attacked by an assailant.

_x_True __False

5. Any gun owner can use deadly force against a threat of deadly force.

_x_True __False

6. It's ok to point my gun at someone else if it isn't loaded.

__True _x_False

7. Little children can hold and handle a real weapon as long as an adult supervises them.

__True _x_False

8. "Muscle Memory" is the ability to remember what hand musceles to use in gripping your weapon.

__True _X_False

9. It is illegal to carry a concealed weapon in your vehicle without a concealed carry license.

__True _X_False

10. Responsible gun owners hold the belief that their weapon is always loaded even when the magazine is missing from the magazine well.

X__True __False

11. Verbal threats are not enough to justify deadly force.

_X_True __False

12. It's ok to carry a concealed firearm into a police station as long as you call ahead and notify them that you are coming.

__True _X_False

13. Dealing with, "What If" Scenarios is not recommended as it will confuse and frighten women gun enthusiasts.

__True _X_False

14. Never leave your weapon unattended.

_X_True __False

15. All family members should know all there is to know so as to prevent firearm accidents.

X_True __False

16. Never use your weapon in an attempt to get even or to settle an argument.

_X_True __False

17. If you are the victim of a home invasion, you should Shoot First & Ask Questions Later.

_X_True __False

18. A safe room is not really necessary if you have a gun.

__True X_False

19. You should always seek out the intruder and attack him before he attacks you.

__True _X_False

20. A home where barking dogs live is safer than one without dogs.

_X_True __False

21. If you have to shoot you should keep shooting until the threat is stopped.

_X_True __False

22. Roll Playing different possible threats is a good strategy for self-defense.

_X_True _False

23. Most home invasions happen between 10 am. and 3 pm.

X_True __False

24. We practice shooting at paper people so we are ready for real burglars.

_X_True __False

25. When faced with a possible gunfight you should escape, if possible, rather than fight because fighting should be your last resort.

_X_True __False

26. You can deter a would-be intruder from breaking in by keeping the television on when you are not at home.

_X_True __False

27. Most burglars are friendly and compassionate when they encounter a homeowner. Be nice and they won't hurt you.

__True X_False

28. Using deadly force requires police approval.

__True _X_False

29. Standing Your Ground and The Castle Doctrine refer to the same thing.

_X_True __False

30. Calling out to an intruder is ok as long as you don't use profanity.

__True _X_False

31. If you think there is an intruder in your home, the very 1st thing you should do is turn the lights on to be sure.

__True _X_False

32. A burglary usually takes less than 3-minutes to rob your home.

_X_True __False

33. 39% of homeowners admit leaving their doors unlocked the same or more as their parents.

_X_True __False

34. Self-defense takes forethought and even thinking on the fly as situations occur.

_X_True __False

35. Being, "Street Smart" is the key to good self-defense.

_X_True __False

CONCLUSION

After many hours of research, interviews and deliberation, I have come to the following conclusions:

1. If only 1 in 1,000 experience a home invasion, the odds are 1,000 to 1 that it will happen to me.

2. If 28% of all home invasions find homeowners at home, there is a 72% chance that I will be out of the house and safe from violence should it ever happen to me.

3. If only 7% experience a violent encounter with an intruder during a home invasion, there is a 93% chance that, should I be home during a home invasion, I will not encounter a violent act of aggression.

4. If only 5.6% of burglaries occur among Senior Citizens, there is a 94.4% chance that it will not happen to me.

5. If most home invasions occur in the top 10 counties of Florida, the odds are even greater that it will not happen to me.

6. If I have been diligent in conducting a Home Safety Inspection and now have a burglar alarm, bolted front door, two barking dogs and multiple loaded handguns ready to go, there is a much less chance of being targeted than if I did nothing.

7. If I continue to fear (Reverence) the Lord, his angel will set up his camp of waring angels all around me to protect me and even deliver me from harm. (Psalm 34:7-9)

The Fear Is Worse Than The Burglary

Those who study these things tell us that our reality is shaped by what we think. The Bible supports this premise. Proverbs 23 says: "For as he thinketh in his heart, so is he." Thoughts always generates feelings that in turn determine actions.

I can remember a story that was told to me when I as a kid. It went like this. There were several men, I guess you would call them tramps, that hung around the trains looking for one that had empty open cargo cars that they could ride.

One night they found such a car. The door was open so they climbed in. Later they learned that the yard master had closed the door and locked it to prevent folks getting into it. It was a refrigerated car and was kept cold at all times.

Long story short, the men began to get cold and thought the temperature was dropping. They convinced themselves that they were going to freeze and would eventually die.

The truth of the matter, that the men didn't know, was the temperature had been set on 60 degrees. Their thoughts led them to believe they would freeze to death…and they did. The next afternoon, the car was opened and they found the men dead.

What you believe shapes your destiny. Logic was not used to think out the situation. They followed their feelings that were generated by their thoughts.

I used to say, "If the flu is going around, I will get it for sure." And I did. Once I began to think what the scriptures say, I stayed free from the flu and other sicknesses. *Isaiah 53:5* says, "But he was wounded for our transgressions, he was bruised for our iniquities: the chastisement of our peace was upon him; and ***with his stripes we*** are ***healed***."

The fear of something happening is far worse than the actual thing you fear. Home invasions and burglaries are no different. Some folks obsess over being a victim and live in a continual state of torment. That is not what Jesus wanted for us. He said, "The thief cometh to steal, *and* to kill, *and* to destroy: I *am come* that *they might have life, and* that *they might have it* more abundantly. John 10:10

The will of God has always been to experience life to its fullest. We accomplish that by faith and believing and applying the promises of God. Did you know that there are over 3,000 promises in the Bible that are yours for the taking?

As Christians, we are called to believe God. When we do, our thoughts align with his promises and our feeling change into an attitude of faith and we begin to live life as God wanted us to live.

If you are trapped in and alternate reality, changing your thought patterns will make all the difference. However, first you must accept the reality you are in. Don't fight it or ignore it. It is what it is. Only time and persistence in believing the truths of the Bible will change your reality. This takes time, prayer and lots of research to discover what the promises of God are.

AUTHOR'S NOTES TO HIS READERS

Post Script.....Where Are They Now?

That's what I was asked when my friends read my manuscript. So, I called each one to see what is going on in their lives today.

Susan is in the county jail for shooting her boyfriend over a matter of eating her hamburger.

Phil went to Australia on a gold hunting expedition with some of his collage friends.

Tom told me he was going to retire in the spring and asked me if I know of a good place to live out his twilight years.

Sarah won the lottery and walked away with over three million dollars after taxes.

Professor Evans is now an evangelist working in the far east with Gospel Light Ministries.

Bill was killed in a car accident last year.

Captain Courageous ran for public office and is now an elected official being one of nine County Commissioners.

Lt. Brooks…was captured by aliens, well, that's what they say anyway. He was never heard of again.

The two burglars were sentenced to five years in the state juvenile detention facility.

Last but not at all least is Benny. He did get his weapons back and continued on in his self-defense training. He is now the court appointed professor that teaches good gun safety and common-sense self-defense.

Oh yeah, the judge. She was replaced by a conservative Republican.

WINNING THE BATTLE

We must use the Word of God
To calm emotions that fray.
For the enemy never sleeps,
Until he has led us astray.

So when your emotions overflow
With feelings like depression and fear.
Know this! If you dwell in that place,
You invite the enemy to draw near.

When your emotions rage
With fiery darts aglow,
Stand in the power of the Lord,
Against its awful woe.

And if you get confused
And lost in the storm,
Put your thoughts on trial,
Rejecting all but heaven born.

You can win the battle
That rages within your soul.
By casting down imaginations,
And breaking Satan's hold.
Remember to focus on Jesus,
Holding the world at arm's length.
Lift up your head above the trial,
And the Lord will give you strength.

By John Marinelli

"For the weapons of our warfare are not carnal but mighty, through God, to the pulling down of strongholds: casting down imaginations and every high thing that exalts itself against the knowledge of God, and bringing into captivity every thought to the obedience of Christ." II Corinthians 10:3-5 The battle is in our minds and we win by putting our thoughts on trial and casting out all that oppose the knowledge of God. This is true victory.

ABOUT THE AUTHOR
JOHN MARINELLI

Rev. Marinelli is an ordained minister, He has formed and been pastor of one church in Wisconsin and was the pastor of another in Alabama. He has also been a youth minister and evangelism director over the years.

Rev. Marinelli has authored several other books including: "Original Story Poems", "The Art of Writing Christian Poetry," "Pulpit Poems," "Moonlight & Mistletoe," "The Mysterious Stranger," "With Eagles Wings," "Mysteries & Miracles," "It Came To Pass," Why Do The Righteous Suffer," "Believer's Handbook of battle Strategies." "Hidden In Plain Sight" "The End of The World, From The Beginning" "Mister Tugboat" "An Elephant Named Clyde" "Morning Reign" "Times Past But Not Forgotten" and "How To Have A Victorious Christian Life."(www.marinellichristianbooks.com)

John is an accomplished Christian poet. He also dabbles in songwriting, likes to play chess, sings karaoke and goes fishing now and then. He lives in north central Florida where he enjoys a retired lifestyle with his wife and two collies.

GLOSSARY OF TERMS

ACCIDENTAL DISCHARGE: A term incorrectly used to identify a negligent discharge. Following the three basic safety rules of handling a firearm is no accident. Not following them can lead to a negligent discharge. Firearms safety is no accident.

AMBIDEXTROUS SAFETY: A manual, external safety that can be easily reached with either hand. It often features dual levers, with one lever on each side of the firearm.

ASSAULT RIFLE: By U.S. Army definition… a selective-fire rifle chambered for a cartridge of intermediate power. If applied to any semi-automatic firearm regardless of its cosmetic similarity to a true assault rifle, the term is incorrect.

AUTOMATIC: A firearm designed to feed cartridges, fire them, eject their empty cases and repeat this cycle as long as the trigger is depressed and cartridges remain in the feed system. Examples: machine guns, sub-machine guns, selective-fire rifles, including true assault rifles.

AUTOMATIC PISTOL: A term used often to describe what is actually a semiautomatic pistol. It is, technically, a misnomer but a near-century of use has legitimized it, and its use confuses only the novice.

CALIBER: The nominal diameter of a projectile of a rifled firearm or the diameter between lands in a rifled barrel. In this country, usually expressed in hundreds of an inch; in Great Britain in thousandths; in Europe and elsewhere in millimeters.

CCW: "Carry Concealed Weapon" To carry a handgun concealed. "Concealed Carry Weapon" A permit/license to carry a concealed firearm.

DOUBLE-ACTION: A handgun mechanism where pulling the trigger retracts and releases the hammer or firing pin to initiate discharge.

DOUBLE ACTION / SINGLE ACTION: DA/SA firearms are designed to operate in *double action* on the initial shot, and in *single action* on the second and subsequent shots. Consequently, these guns tend to have a long, heavy trigger pull for the first shot, and a relatively short and light trigger pull for subsequent shots. This is because the first trigger pull gets the internal parts into position, while the energy from the first shot is used to prep the mechanism for follow-up shots.

DRY FIRING: Aiming and firing the weapon without live ammunition. This is an excellent technique to improve marksmanship skills, however, check with your gun manufacture to be sure it's ok for the type of gun you own. It can cause damage to certain weapons.

EJECTION PORT: The opening through which the empty, spent ammunition case is cast out of a firearm.

EXTERNAL SAFETY: A safety that is placed on the outer surfaces of the firearm and is accessible to the user. Not all external safeties require user attention. For instance, a grip safety is an external safety, but requires no deliberate act on the part of the shooter in order to do its job.

FAILURE TO EXTRACT: A semi-automatic firearm malfunction in which the extractor fails to yank the old case out of the way as the slide travels back, so the spent case is still in the chamber as the slide on its return journey tries to stuff the new round into the same space. A failure to extract often causes a double feed malfunction.

FAILURE TO FEED …A semi-automatic firearm malfunction in which the slide passes entirely over the fresh round, failing to pick it up to insert in the chamber as the slide returns to battery. Failures-to-feed and misfeeds are closely related malfunctions, and the two problems often share a root cause.

FAILURE TO FIRE: Any malfunction which results in nothing happening when the trigger is pulled. Most commonly caused by a failure to feed the ammunition properly into the chamber, a failure to fire can also be caused by bad ammunition or by a broken firing pin.

FIRING PIN: The part of the breech mechanism that strikes the primer of the cartridge.

FLINCH: To move or jerk a firearm involuntarily while shooting.

FOLLOW-THROUGH: The continued mental and physical application of marksmanship fundamentals after each round has been fired.

HANGFIRE: Extended delay (up to a second or more) between the firing pin blow and the ignition of the powder, usually caused by old or contaminated primer/propellant which ignites slower than usual.

1. Keep the muzzle pointed in a safe direction.
2. Count 75 to ten SLOWLY.
3. With the opening in the action pointed away from your face, eject the cartridge and examine it
4. Attempt to determine the cause of the failure.

HIGH-CAPACITY MAGAZINE: An inexact, non-technical term indicating a magazine holding more rounds than might be considered "average."

JACKET: The envelope enclosing the core of a bullet.

JAM: A malfunction which locks up the gun so badly that tools are required in order to fix it. Sometimes used to denote a simple malfunction, but many people do make a distinction between a complete jam and a simple malfunction.

LASER: As used around firearms, a laser is an alternative sighting device similar to a laser pointer, which enables the shooter to quickly and accurately see where the firearm is aimed even when lighting or other conditions preclude being able to use the gun's normal sights. Lasers may be located within or hung from accessory rails at the front end of the gun, or even placed within the firearm itself as part of the guide rod.

MAGAZINE: A spring-loaded container for cartridges that may be an integral part of the gun's mechanism or may be detachable. Detachable magazines for the same gun may be offered by the gun's manufacturer or other manufacturers with various capacities. A gun with a five-shot detachable magazine, for instance, may be fitted with a magazine holding 10, 20, or 50 or more rounds. Box magazines are most commonly located under the receiver with the cartridges stacked vertically. Tube or tubular magazines run through the stock or under the barrel with the cartridges lying horizontally. Drum magazines hold their cartridges in a circular mode. A magazine can also mean a secure storage place for ammunition or explosives.

MAGNUM: A term indicating a relatively heavily loaded metallic cartridge or shot shell and, by extension, a gun safely constructed to fire it.

MAINSPRING: A strong spring, aka an energy storage device that operates the striker or hammer of a firearm.

MANUAL SAFETY: A safety which the shooter must deliberately disengage in order to fire the gun. All manual safeties are also external safeties, but not all external safeties are manual safeties as well.

MISFEED: In semi-automatic firearms, a failure of the next round to completely enter the chamber. A misfeed can keep the gun from going into battery, which in turn may prevent the gun from firing. Misfeeds and failures to feed are closely related: a failure to feed is a round that never even leaves the top of the magazine, while a misfeed is a round that leaves the magazine but does not enter the chamber.

MUZZLE: The open end of the barrel from which the projectile exits.

OUT OF BATTERY: The condition where the breeching mechanism is not in proper position for firing.

PASSIVE SAFETY: Any safety, internal or external, which functions apart from the shooter's conscious control. Grip safeties are one example of a passive external safety; drop safeties are an example of a passive internal safety.

PLINKING: Informal shooting at any of a variety of inanimate targets. The most often practiced shooting sport in this country.

POINT SHOOTING: Shooting without using the sights. Instead of using sights, point shooters use body position or other cues to provide a rough index of where the shots will land. Point shooting is a source of much controversy in the shooting community, especially online.

PRIMER: The ignition component of a cartridge generally made up of a metallic fulminate or (currently) lead styphnate.

PRINTING: A condition in which the outline of the concealed handgun may be discerned through the outer clothing. The firearm itself is not visible, but its presence and shape may be readily apparent to an observer.

RACKING THE SLIDE: A semi-automatic term that means pulling the slide back to its rearmost position, and then letting it go forward under its own spring tension. If the magazine is loaded and inserted in the gun, racking the slide loads the chamber and prepares the gun to fire.

RIMFIRE: A rimmed or flanged cartridge with the priming mixture located inside the rim of the case. The most famous example is the .22 rim fire. It has been estimated that between 3-4 billion .22 cartridges are loaded in the U.S. each year.

SAFETY: A device that blocks the firing mechanism of a firearm.

SATURDAY NIGHT SPECIAL: a pejorative or slang term used in the United States for any inexpensive handgun. It is sometimes called an SNS in written shorthand. Traditionally, Saturday night specials have often been defined as compact, inexpensive handguns with a barrel length of under three inches (for pistols, overall length of under six inches) and low perceived quality, although there is no official definition of "Saturday night special" under any federal or state law.

SAWED-OFF SHOTGUN (RIFLE): Common term for federally restricted "short-barreled shotgun (rifle)" i.e. a conventional shotgun with barrel less than 18" (rifle less than 16") or overall length less than 26."

SEMI-AUTOMATIC: A firearm designed to fire a single cartridge, eject the empty case and reload the chamber each time the trigger is pulled.

SIGHT ALIGNMENT: The manner in which the sights are lined up properly in front of the shooter's eye, to form a straight path to the target at the moment the trigger is pulled.

SIGHT PICTURE: What the shooter sees when looking through the sights at the target at the moment the trigger is pulled.

SNUB-NOSED: Descriptive of (usually) a revolver with an unusually short barrel.

SLIDE LOCK: When most semi-automatic firearms have been fired until empty, the slide will remain in its rearmost position rather than going forward as if to chamber another round. This condition of the gun is called slide lock.

SLIDE RELEASE: The slide release lever, usually located on the left side of the slide, is pushed down to unlock the slide and allow the slide to move forward into its normal position. It is sometimes called the slide stop or slide stop lever.

SLIDE STOP: The slide release lever.

STAGGERED COLUNM MAGAZINE: A box magazine that has two staggered columns of cartridges that increase capacity but not length of the magazine.

STOVEPIPE: Malfunction occurring when a case gets stuck between the breech face and the slide.

STRIKER FIRED: A striker is a form of firing pin that replaces the hammer and firing pin with a single unit. So a striker-fired handgun is a semi-automatic that uses a striker, rather than a hammer or a firing pin, to hit the primer and fire the round.

SUBMACHINE GUN: An automatic firearm commonly firing pistol ammunition intended for close-range combat.

TAP, RACK, BANG: The slang term for the procedure to clear a misfeed. To clear a misfeed, tap the base of the magazine firmly to be sure it is properly seated, rack the slide to eject an empty case or feed a new round, and assess to be sure your target still needs shooting. If it does, bang.

TRIGGER: The part of a firearm mechanism that releases the firing pin.

TRIGGER GUARD: A metal loop around the trigger designed to protect it.

TRIGGER PULL: The entire process of moving the trigger from its forward most position to its rearward most position, causing the hammer to fall and the shot to fire.

TRIGGER PULL WEIGHT: How much pressure the trigger finger must put on the trigger before the gun will fire. Trigger pull weight is measured in pounds and ounces.

TRIGGER SAFETY: An external, passive safety that can be found on the face of some trigger designs (most notably found on Glock firearms). It is intended to prevent the trigger from being pulled by objects that find their way into the trigger guard area.

WEAPON: Webster defines it as "an instrument of offensive or defensive combat." Thus an automobile, baseball bat, bottle, chair, firearm, fist, penknife or shovel is a "weapon," if so used.

WEAVER STANCE: In the Weaver stance, the body is angled slightly in relation to the target rather than squarely facing it. The elbows are flexed and pointed downward. The strong-side arm is slightly straighter than the weak-side arm. The shooter pushes out with the gun hand, while the weak hand pulls back. This produces a push-pull tension, which is the chief defining characteristic of the Weaver stance.

(More books by John Marinelli can be viewed and purchased from his website: www.marinellichristianbooks.com)